The Kindhearted Crocodile

by Lucia Panzieri

illustrated by
AntonGionata Ferrari

Holiday House / New York

Library of Congress Cataloging-in-Publication Data

Panzieri, Lucia.

[Coccodrillo gentile. English]

The kindhearted crocodile / by Lucia Panzieri ; illustrated by AntonGionata Ferrari. — 1st ed.

JUN 1 1 2013   p. cm.

Summary: A crocodile that longs to be a pet sneaks into a house,

hides in the pages of a picture book during the day, and comes out at night

to do kind and useful things for the family while they sleep.

ISBN 978-0-8234-2767-3 (hardcover)

[1. Crocodiles as pets — Fiction.]

I. Ferrari, Antongionata, 1960 - ill. II. Title.

PZ7.P1952Kin 2013

[E]—dc23

2012025486

To Luigi and Teresa,
the beginning of everything
—L. P.

To Tiziana, Alvise,
and Sofia, gentle crocodiles
—AG. F.

Once upon a time there was a crocodile with big, sharp teeth; powerful jaws; and a swift, strong body—everything he needed to be the most fearsome creature you could imagine.

But the story goes that this crocodile had a very kind heart. He was a gentle and sensitive soul who longed to live in a home and to play with children. His great dream was to be a pet— like a puppy or a goldfish—and to spend his days as a companion to a happy family.

And he would make such a good pet, for he knew how to push a swing, how to dance on a rope, and how to bake an apple pie.

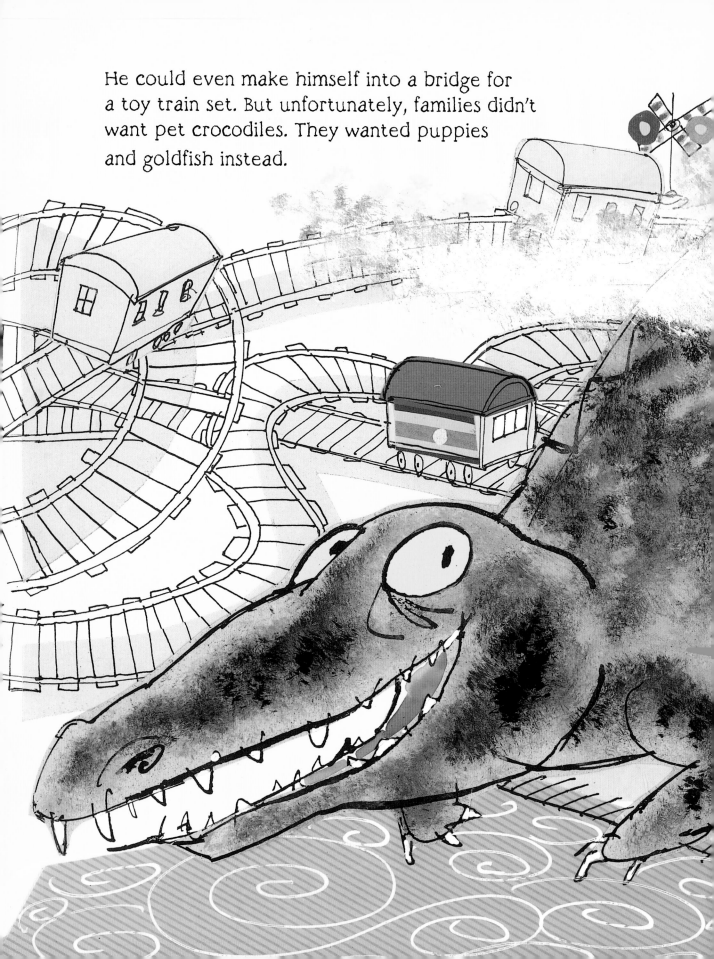

He could even make himself into a bridge for a toy train set. But unfortunately, families didn't want pet crocodiles. They wanted puppies and goldfish instead.

Then the kindly crocodile had a brilliant idea. He would sneak into a home through the pages of a lovely picture book. Inside the book he was just paper and paint.

But at night he crept off the pages and into the house, where he performed many kind and useful tasks to prove that he was the perfect pet.

He tidied toys.

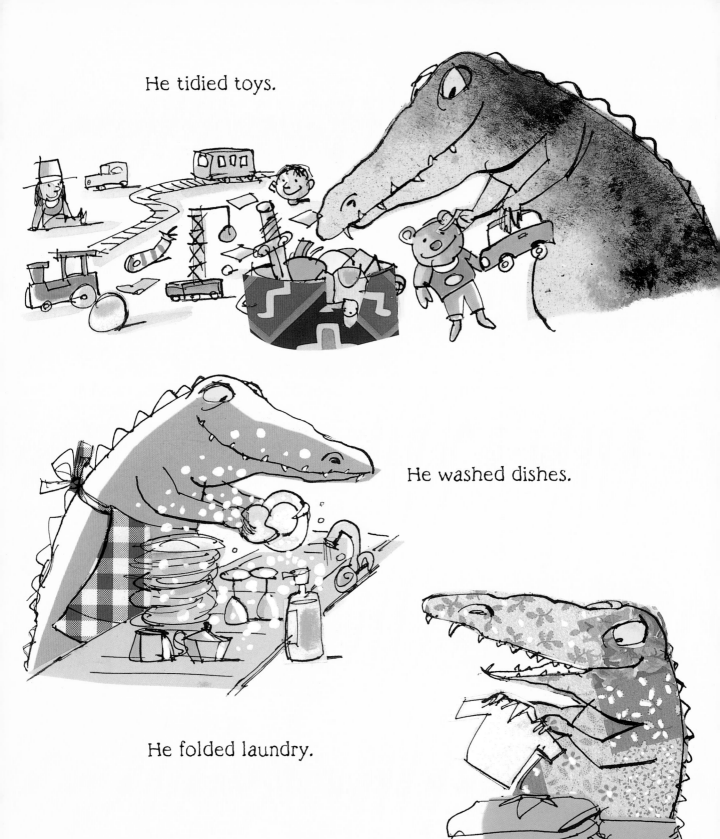

He washed dishes.

He folded laundry.

He fought monsters in bad dreams.

And as dawn approached, he spread sweet jam
on toast for the family's breakfast.

When morning came, the kindly crocodile, ever so silently and quite reluctantly, returned to the illustrations in the picture book.

The Kindhearted Crocodile

by Lucia Panzieri
illustrated by
ntonGionata Ferrari

Meanwhile, the family wondered, *Who is tidying the toys? Who is washing dishes and folding laundry? Who is chasing away our nightmares and making our breakfast?*

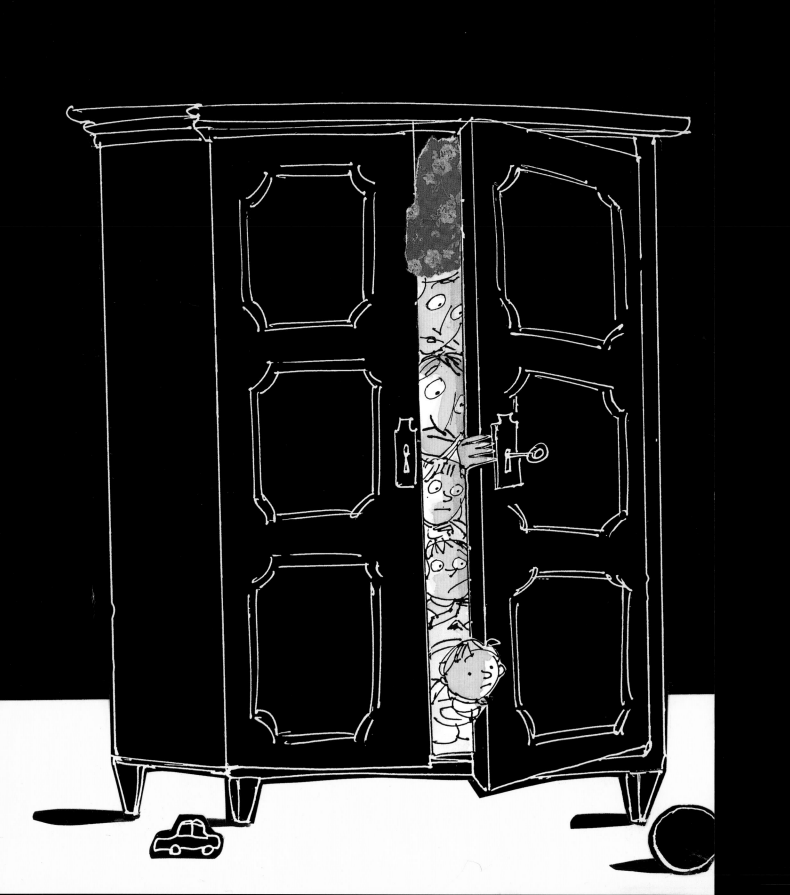

They thought they would see a fairy, a troll,
a wizard, or an elf.

That's why one night the father, the mother,
and the children squeezed themselves into a
wardrobe to wait for their secret friend.

a ferocious-looking crocodile with a long, strong
body and an enormous mouth with dozens of
sharp, pointy teeth.

"Help! Call the fire department!"
said the frantic mother.

"Not to worry. I will fight him,"
said the courageous father.

The children, who already knew and loved
the crocodile from their picture book, cried,
"We want to keep him."

Meanwhile, the kindly crocodile swiftly slipped
between his covers.

Later that night,
the mother and father had
a serious conversation. The
mother, who appreciated
help with dishes and
laundry, overcame her initial
fear and now agreed with
the children.

But the father had as many doubts
as the crocodile had teeth.

Then morning came. And the crocodile, who had learned a great deal about the likes and dislikes of the family he longed to live with, fixed a very good cup of coffee for each of the grown-ups.

"Thank you," said the father. "You are very kind indeed. And this is excellent coffee. You may stay with us for a few days."

And guess what! If you visit the family today,
the crocodile is still with them!